THE CREEPY CLASSICS

CHILDREN'S COLLECTION

Dados Internacionais de Catalogação na Publicação (CIP) de acordo com ISBD

S545f Shelley, Mary.
Frankenstein / Mary Shelley. - Jandira, SP : W. Books, 2025
120 p. ; 12,80cm x 19,80cm. - (Classics).

ISBN: 978-65-5294-189-3

1. Literatura inglesa. 2. Terror. 3. Clássicos. 4. Fantasia. 5. Imaginação. 6. Suspense.
I. Título. II. Série.

2025-2535 CDD 823.91
CDU 821.111-3

Elaborada por Lucio Feitosa - CRB-8/8803
Índice para catálogo sistemático:
1. Literatura inglesa 823.91
2. Literatura inglesa 821.111-3

The Creepy Classics Collection

Text based on the original story by Mary Shelley,
adapted by Gemma Barder
Illustrations by Nick Moffatt

1st edition in 2025
www.cirandacultural.com.br

FRANKENSTEIN

MARY SHELLEY

W. Books

THE CREATURE

Victor's experiment

VICTOR FRANKENSTEIN

A student of science and nature

ELIZA

Victor's friend
and sweetheart

HENRY

Victor's friend

WILLIAM

Victor's younger brother

Chapter One

My name is Victor Frankenstein.

I grew up in a beautiful town called Geneva, in Switzerland. I lived with my mother, father and little brother, William. When I was eight years old, my family agreed to look after an orphan called Eliza. Eliza was only a few years younger than William and I, and we instantly became friends.

Our childhood was filled with love and laughter.

Eliza, William and I spent endless days exploring the woods just beyond the gates of Geneva with our friend, Henry. There, the three of us developed an interest in nature. We collected samples of plants and flowers to take home, and we were fascinated with the animals who built their homes among the trees.

As I grew, I read more and more about the natural world. I took out every book our library had on nature. Most of all, I became obsessed with discovering *how* life was created. How did a flower grow and bloom? How did a bird grow inside its egg? When did the spark of life begin and what gave it its power?

One evening, a great storm swirled around our house. Eliza and William were scared and hid under their duvets, but I wanted to watch. This was nature at its most powerful, after all. A huge bolt of lightning struck our chimney and destroyed part of the stack. Bricks tumbled to the ground leaving a scorched hole in their place. I was shocked but excited by the power that lightning held.

Gradually, Henry, William and Eliza spent less time in the woods, but I still loved to explore the natural world. I applied to all the top universities in Europe to study science so that I might learn the answers to all the questions in my head.

Life was perfect, until the day my beloved mother became ill. None of the treatments or medicines the doctors prescribed could save her. I watched as the spark of life that had always burnt so brightly inside her grew dimmer and dimmer. One day, it went out completely.

Chapter Two

After my mother died, I became more determined than ever to understand life and its cause. I wanted to find out all I could about that spark of energy that makes us all live and breathe. Perhaps if I understood it, I could prevent what had happened to my mother from happening to anyone else I loved.

When the time came to leave for university, I said a tearful goodbye to Eliza. By then she was more to me than just a childhood friend. I was in love. But I wanted to build a life and become someone worthy of her before I thought of marriage.

Henry planned to travel Europe before beginning his studies, and William stayed behind in Geneva to look after our father. And so, leaving everyone I knew behind, I set off for Germany, to a town called Ingolstadt. The university there was filled with the brightest minds in Europe.

I paid close attention in all my lectures and I even devoted my spare time to learning.

'Young man, I see you in this library more than any other student here at Ingolstadt,' said a voice as I worked in the library late one night. 'Don't you want to go and have some fun with your classmates?'

Looking up from my books, I realised that it was Professor Waldman. I smiled politely. 'Thank you, sir, but I am not here to have fun. I am here to study.'

The professor stroked his grey moustache thoughtfully. 'I see you have a keen interest in nature and biology,' he said.

'Yes, sir,' I replied. 'I want to study life. I want to understand how it is created. What gives life its power.'

The professor looked at me closely for a moment or two. 'Follow me,' he said. Before I could agree, he disappeared among the high rows of dusty book shelves. I followed him to a dark corner of the library that smelt of damp.

'Ah, here it is,' said Professor Waldman, handing me a large, leatherbound book. 'I don't recommend this one very often. Not many of my students have the imagination to understand it – but I believe you will find it most interesting.'

I thanked the professor and tucked the book under my arm. I did not want to be rude, but I already had a stack of books to read and did not think I needed another. The professor nodded and wished me good night. I thought no more about the book until I got back to my apartment that evening.

The student apartments at Ingolstadt were small but comfortable. As well as a bedroom with a desk to work at, each of the science students had a small, private laboratory to conduct our own experiments.

Although I was tired from a full day of studying, something about the book Professor Waldman gave

laboratory
A place used for scientific investigation and experiments.

me drew me to open it. I lifted the heavy cover and leafed through the fragile pages, crisp and yellow with age. Inside were some of the strangest experiments and ideas I had ever come across. There were long chapters on how scientists had created life in their own laboratories by using the power of nature. With wind, water and, occasionally, lightning.

My mind began to fizz with excitement. I had already witnessed the power that lightning held. It was enough to destroy bricks and mortar. It made our hair stand on end and the very air around us crackle. The idea that it could be used to create life made sense to me.

I read on. Before I knew it, the sun was rising and birds were chattering outside my window. I had spent the entire night reading the old book from cover to cover. Now, I was ready to put my new knowledge to the test.

Chapter Three

As the months at university passed by, I continued to attend my lectures and complete each task set for me by my professors. Afterwards, I would rush to my own laboratory and carry on the work I had started.

At first, my experiments were small, but my progress was fast. In particular, I studied the human body in all its stages of life and death. I shared many of my findings with Professor Waldman, but he was not the only one impressed by my work. I was beginning to make a name for myself at the university. More importantly, I was getting closer to my secret goal: I was going to make my own creature – one capable of thinking and feeling – and bring it to life.

As I progressed, I shared less and less with the professors. I even bought a lock for my laboratory, in case anyone stumbled across my work and wanted to steal it. Then I shut myself away to start building my creation.

I was so lost in my work that I had no time to answer the pile of letters I received from Father and Eliza, or the postcards Henry sent me from his travels. I was on the brink of making a discovery that could possibly change the world!

After weeks and weeks of work, without a word to anyone, my creature was almost ready. It lay on my laboratory table, still and silent. In the darkness, it almost looked human, but it was far taller than any human I had ever met. I dressed it in my old clothes, but they were cropped and small around the creature's big arms and legs.

There was only one part of my experiment left to complete. The part that I had been studying for my entire life. The part that filled me with fear and excitement all at once. I wanted to give my creature the spark of life, but to do that I needed the greatest power in nature – *lightning*.

It took agonising weeks of waiting and sleepless nights, but finally a storm was forecast for the skies over Ingolstadt. At midnight, when my fellow students were sheltering in their beds, I opened up my laboratory windows. Carefully, I set up my equipment to channel the lightning. From there the energy would fill my creature and, if my experiment worked, bring it to life.

Chapter Four

The storm raged outside my laboratory windows. I could see lightning strikes illuminating the town, but none had come close to my building. Just as I began to think that my equipment would not work and my experiment would fail, I heard a loud crack and my laboratory filled with light. I shielded my eyes against the brightness as sparks shot around the room. I looked at the creature on my table. It seemed to crackle all over, but as the flash faded, it remained still and unmoving.

The experiment had not worked.

With a disappointed sigh, I began to put the instruments around the laboratory away. But something drew my eye back to the table. A movement. Small, like a breath of wind against a curtain.

I stared at the creature. Was it a trick of the light? No. Its finger twitched again, as though it was nudging away a fly. I stepped closer and could see without a doubt that its chest was rising and falling. It was breathing!

'Ngruh …'

I jumped back as the creature let out a deep groan. It was alive! I was filled with joy as I realised my achievement. I had harnessed the spark of life and created a living, breathing thing!

The creature groaned again as it shifted its arms and legs. 'That's it,' I whispered. 'Keep going.' The creature then sat upright, its legs dangling off the edge of the table in the trousers that were far too short. 'I did it,' I said to myself. 'I did it!'

The creature finally opened its eyes and looked straight at me.

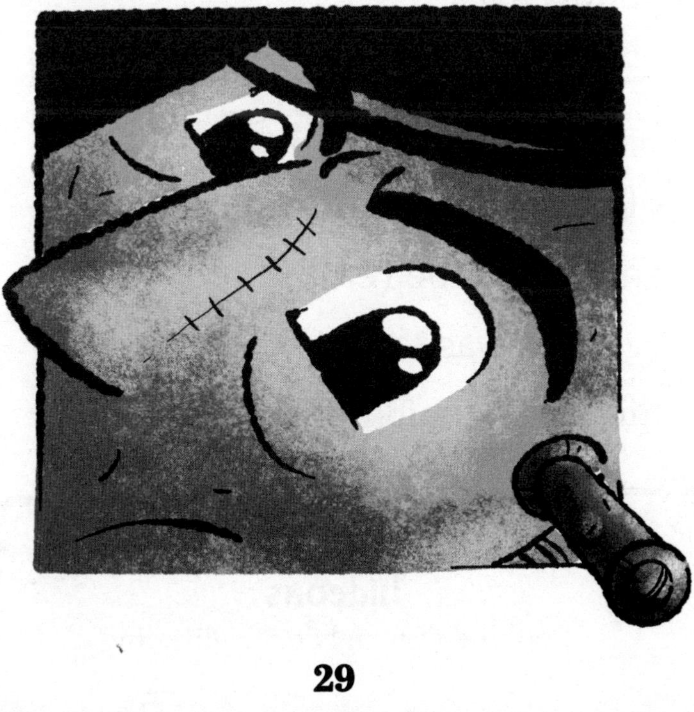

A wave of sickness rolled through my stomach. I stared, finally taking in what I had done. I no longer saw my success. I saw the creature's dry yellow skin and black lips. Its long, lumbering arms and legs. The dead look in its yellow eyes …

'What have I done?' I muttered. 'I have gone against all the laws of nature. This hideous creature should not be real!'

But it was too late. I had created life, and I could not reverse the

hideous
Looking very ugly or frightening.

experiment. I began to tremble as the creature stood and towered over me. It was still staring as though waiting for me to do something. What I did was run. Terrified of my own creation, I ran out of my apartment, and into the night.

***

I wandered the streets of Ingolstadt, feeling like a child whose dream had turned into a nightmare. My mind raced with the horror of what I had done. What would Professor Waldman think of me? What would my *family* think of me?

As night turned into early morning, I shivered with cold. But I could not face returning to my apartment – or to the creature.

A warm hand on my shoulder startled me.

'Victor? Is that you?' said a familiar voice. It was Henry, my childhood friend. 'Why on earth are you out here in the street at this time of the morning?'

I hugged my old friend with the last of my strength. Then the exhaustion of the past weeks

of work, and the shock of the previous night, caught up with me.

I sagged against him and would have fallen if his arms had not held me up.

'What is the matter, old friend?' laughed Henry. 'Didn't you get my postcard? I wrote to tell you I am starting my studies here!' He seemed to notice that something was very wrong, and his cheerfulness turned to worry. 'We should get you home,' he said.

CHAPTER FIVE

With my arm around Henry's shoulders, I dragged myself back to my building.

'Before we go inside,' I said. 'I must tell you that I have done something. I have *created* something ...' But I could not find the words to tell Henry what I had done.

'I'm sure everything will be fine,' said Henry, calmly. 'But Victor, your door is open – did you forget to close it? I hope you haven't been burgled.'

I was certain I had closed the door when I fled my apartment the previous night. I remember it banging shut behind me. Fear flooded me again as I imagined someone entering and discovering my horrible experiment. With a surge of nervous energy, I ran into the apartment. It was empty. The laboratory was empty too. The creature had either been taken or had disappeared.

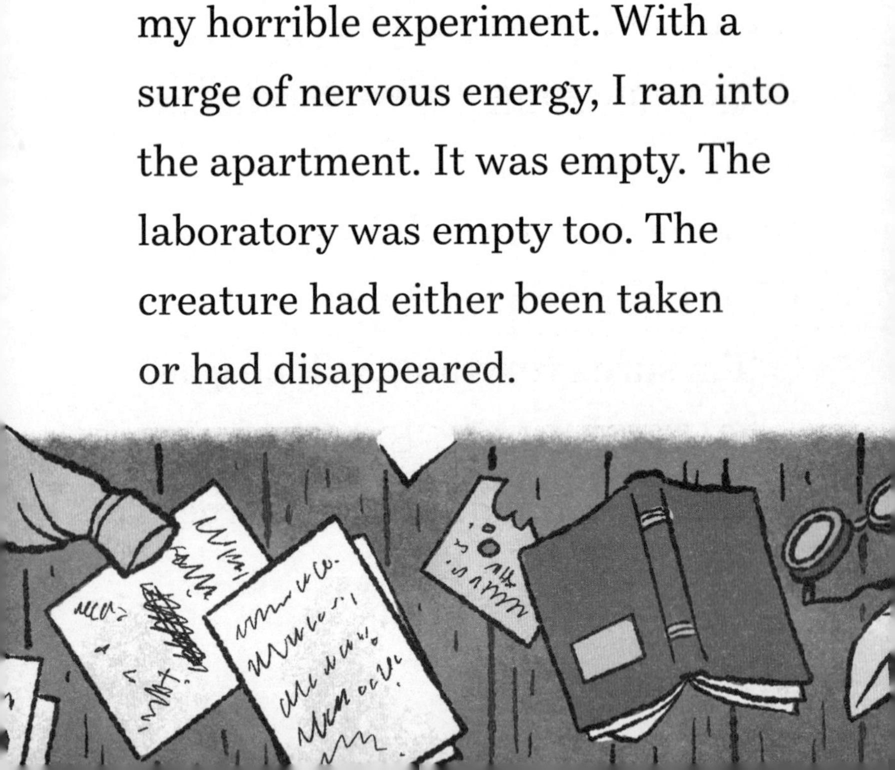

'What is the matter, Victor?' asked Henry, his eyes scanning my messy apartment. I had devoted every hour to my creature, which meant that I'd had no time for cleaning up. Piles of papers and dirty clothes cluttered the room.

'I … I don't think I am very well,' I said at last. 'I think I've had a sort of fever for many weeks. I have not been thinking straight.'

Henry stepped towards me and placed an arm around my shoulders. 'Everything is going

to be all right, my friend,' he said kindly. 'I'm here now.'

***

Henry stayed in Ingolstadt for many months. He started his studies at the business school and asked his professors if he could move in with me. I was very thankful for his help. He tidied my apartment, cooked me food and took me for walks when I was strong enough. I was still too ashamed to tell him what had really happened the night before he found me wandering the streets. What would he have thought of me and the madness that had taken me over?

I had not seen the creature again, and I was grateful. At first, I listened for word that someone had discovered it. When none came, I assumed it had left of its own accord and watched out of my apartment window in case it returned. Each day I feared seeing the large, strange figure appear.

But time passed with no such sighting, and I began to feel that I could put the whole incident behind me.

I destroyed my notes and dismantled my equipment so that all that was left of the creature was my memory of its horrifying face and that deep, terrifying moan. In time, even that began to fade.

Chapter Six

'What a beautiful morning!' said Henry as he entered our apartment. It was six months since he had moved in. 'I've already been to the bakery, dropped off an essay at university and picked up our letters from the post box.'

I smiled at my old friend. Henry never seemed to run out of positivity, and his good mood had made me feel better each and every day. A few weeks after my experiment, I'd been well enough to go back to university and continue my studies. I returned Professor Walden's book, but I did not talk to him about it or what I had done with the knowledge it contained. Instead, I turned my mind to my regular studies – to my future life as a doctor of science. Someone worthy of marrying Eliza.

I looked through the letters Henry had passed me and was overjoyed to see an envelope with Eliza's handwriting on it. I had slowly started to write to my family again, explaining that I had been ill. To me, this did not feel like a lie. I *must* have been ill to have ever thought creating that creature – that *monster* – was a good idea.

I pushed all thoughts of the creature to the back of my mind as I opened Eliza's letter.

Dear Victor,

It is so good to hear from you at last! I am writing to ask you to come home to Geneva as soon as you can. Your brother, William, is missing and your father is very worried. They ask if you can come at once to help them. Please come!

Your loving friend,
Eliza

'William!' I gasped, tossing the letter aside and rushing to my bedroom.

'Whatever is the matter?' asked Henry. 'Is it bad news?'

'My brother is missing,' I said,

frantically packing a bag. 'I must travel to Geneva at once!'

Henry looked concerned. 'Of course. Do not worry about a thing,' he said. 'I shall tell the university where you have gone.'

As I flew out of the door to head to Ingolstadt's train station, Henry called after me. 'Good luck, Victor!'

***

My childhood home in Geneva was always a happy place. It was where I had felt safe and calm, where sunshine streamed through the windows and William, Eliza and I were loved. That day, however, I felt a cold heaviness in the air as I stepped through the familiar front door and hung up my coat and hat. The ticking of the hall clock echoed loudly. I heard footsteps, and Eliza was soon in my arms.

'Thank goodness you are here!' she said, hugging me tightly. She took me by the hand and led me into the living room

where my father was sitting, staring into the fire. He looked much older than when I had left for university a year before. His worry for William filled his face.

I sat down as Father explained what had happened.

'William left for school as usual,' Father began. 'He has been studying very hard, hoping to follow you to Ingolstadt next year.' He paused and took a deep breath. 'But then he did not come home. Someone says they saw him walking in the woods, others say he was in town. We have searched and searched both places. It is as though he has vanished into thin air.'

I laid my hand on his shoulder. 'I am here now,' I reassured him. 'Together, we will find William.'

Chapter Seven

The following morning, I got up early, determined to find William. To my surprise, Eliza was already awake and dressed.

'I had a feeling you would be up,' she said, handing me a cup of tea. 'Are you going to look for William?'

'He must be somewhere,' I replied.

'And I know him better than anyone. I know the places where we used to play as children.'

Eliza looked down. 'I played there, too, Victor,' she said. 'I have been out each day with your father and the police, showing them all our old hideouts. He's like my little brother, too, remember.'

I sighed and placed an arm around Eliza as she started to cry. 'I'm sorry, Eliza,' I said. 'I wasn't thinking. I did not mean to suggest that you hadn't looked properly. But I must do something. I must try to find William.'

From my parents' house, I walked swiftly to the forest beyond the town walls. I knew the pathways so well from my childhood, the hidden shortcuts and the hollowed-out trees we used as hideouts. I searched for hours, not stopping to rest or eat.

As the sun began to lower over the horizon, I realised I had nothing to show for my day.

Just as I set off on the path back to town, I heard movement behind me. I whipped around to see where it had come from. Nothing. Silence. Then again, the distinctive rustling of leaves and the crack of twigs underfoot.

'William!' I called. 'William is that you?'

'It is not William,' said a low, gruff voice.

I scanned the trees, searching for any trace of where the voice may have come from. It chilled me to my very bones. It was familiar somehow, and yet not of this world.

‘Who … who is there?’ I called into the distance.

Then, I saw it. A large, looming, horrible sight – one I had prayed never to see again.

My monster was standing in front of me. I felt dizzy. Cold sweat ran down my spine as I backed away from it.

'No, no, it can't be,' I spluttered. 'How are you here?'

'I can explain everything, if you let me,' said the creature. I had been so shocked to see the creature that it was only then I realised it was *talking* to me. Its voice was low and husky, but it was using words like a real human.

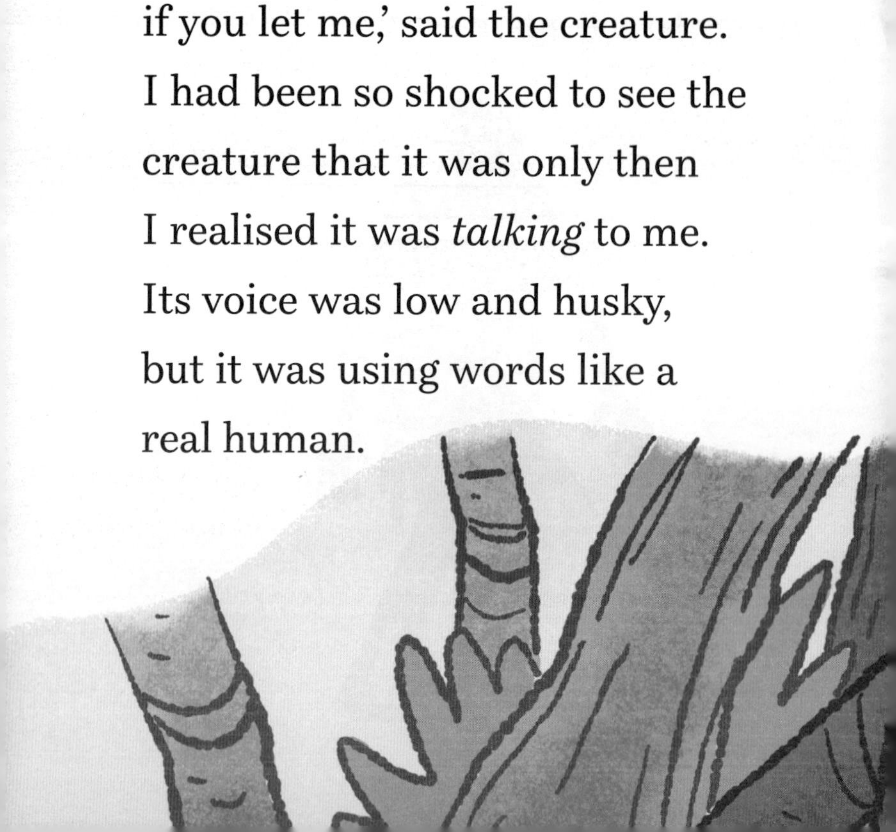

‘Y-you can talk!’ I said, trembling and rooted to the spot.

The creature nodded its black-haired head. ‘Sit with me. I want to tell you my story,’ it said, pointing a withered fingertip towards a clearing. My legs somehow carried me to the spot. I listened, stunned, as the creature spoke.

Chapter Eight

'The first time I opened my eyes, I saw you,' the creature began. 'You had a look of horror on your face. Of course, I did not know what horror was at the time. I did not know anything apart from that I was alive. I could move. I could see. But I did not know who I was.

'When you left me, I tried to follow you into the streets. But the town was confusing. Whenever I saw another human like you, they would scream and run away, or try to attack me. So I headed away from where the people were, into the forest.

'I satisfied the strange feeling in my stomach by eating fruit from trees. I came across a campfire and realised how good it felt to be warm. Slowly, I began to learn what I needed to survive in the world.'

The creature paused, and I looked at it with pity. I had been so scared of what I had done that I had not stopped to think about how the creature itself would feel. It knew nothing of the world – only that I, its creator, had left it.

'One day,' it continued, 'I came across a cottage. I hid in the attached shed for shelter, and I found that I enjoyed watching the family inside. At first, there was only an old man and his son and daughter. They had fallen on hard times, but still they cared for each other, laughed with each other, ate meals together. In them I saw the good that mankind was capable of. Until then, I had experienced only cruelty. They were joined later by a young woman who seemed to know them but did not speak their language. Her lessons were

my lessons, and with her I learnt to speak French.

'I thought of them as 'my cottagers'. Throughout the long, cold winter, I cut firewood for them and left it outside their door. And yet my cottagers did not look like me. *No one* I had come across looked like me at all. My biggest wish was to enjoy the closeness and warmth this family shared.

'When the cottage was empty, I would find a way inside and borrow books from their shelves. Gradually, I taught myself to read.'

I was astounded. The creature had managed to do in six months what most humans take years to achieve! And it was not finished yet.

'I studied geography, history and religion,' the creature added. 'Eventually, I made a plan to introduce myself to my cottagers …'

Chapter Nine

'The father of the family had a problem with his eyes,' the creature explained. 'He wore dark glasses and his family would guide him from room to room. I thought that if he could not see what I looked like, he would not run away from me as most other humans had.'

'I waited until he was alone, then I knocked on the cottage door. I was filled with joy when the old man answered and did not look at me in horror. I told him I was lost, and he invited me in for tea. He was the first human I had ever spoken to. To spend time with someone like that was a dream. I enjoyed myself so much that I did not notice the rest of the family return. When they saw me in their living room, they screamed. I fled.

'I was torn between sadness and anger, but I knew that I could not stay in the shed by the cottage any longer. I would never be welcomed by my cottagers. I needed to find somewhere else. You gave me these clothes when you made me,' the creature said, looking down at the ragged clothes I had given him. The arms and legs seemed even shorter now, dirty and torn. 'There was a letter in the pocket. The address was a place called Geneva, which I had seen on maps.'

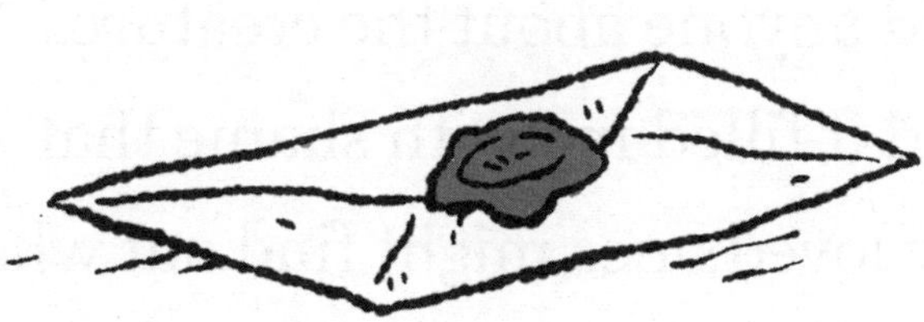

I suddenly felt cold all over. The creature had come here on purpose.

'Why?' I asked, my mouth dry. 'Why would you come here?'

'Because you created me. You are the only family I know. You did not want me, but I thought perhaps your family would be kind to me instead.'

'You met my family?' I asked, jumping up in terror. I had never told anyone about the creature, and it filled me with shame that my loved ones might find out what I had done.

'No,' replied the creature. 'I got as far as the woods outside the town when I saw a young man. He looked just like you.'

'William!' I gasped. 'What happened to him? What did you do?'

The creature looked at me with its cold, dead eyes and continued speaking. 'As I drew nearer, I realised that he wasn't you, but he had already seen me by then. He was terrified. Just like you when you saw

me for the first time. Just like my cottagers.'

'What happened to William?' I shouted.

The creature's eyes bored into mine. I could not read them. 'He tried to run, so I held onto him. I just wanted him to stay.

I told him you had created me, but he did not believe me. He screamed louder. He did not want to listen! I was filled with anger. If I could not be part of your family, then why should he?'

'You killed him!' I realised.

The creature nodded.

I fell to my knees in the mud. 'I wish I had never made you!' I wept. 'Leave me be! Leave this town and never return!'

But the creature stayed where it was, staring at me, still and silent.

'I will leave you on one condition,' it said at last. 'You made me, but I am alone in this world. It is impossible for me to have the warmth and love shared by a family because no one will accept me. All I want is someone like me to spend my days with.'

I stepped back in horror. The creature was asking me to make another monster just like him. The very thought of it filled me with dread.

'I will not do it!' I said.

'You will!' commanded the creature in a loud, gravelly voice that made my hair stand on end. 'If you do not, I will follow you wherever you go. But create one living soul that does not hate me, and I will leave you and all other humans alone.'

There was a moment of silence. All I could hear was the creature's breath.

'After all,' it said at last, 'it is your fault I exist. You must be the one to put things right.'

My mind raced. What could I do? If I left the creature alone in the woods and did nothing, it would follow me. It would come for my family and my secret would be revealed. What would my dear Eliza think of me? Or my father? I pictured their faces as they saw the creature, and a wave of despair crashed over me.

'All right,' I said, my shoulders drooping. 'I will make another creature for you. But you must promise me to disappear forever. You must *never* come near me or my family again. Agreed?'

'Agreed.'

Chapter Ten

'My dear boy, you have only just got here!' said my father. 'You can't be leaving already.'

I packed my bags in silence. 'Please tell Eliza that I have gone,' I said, quietly. 'I cannot bear to say goodbye to her.'

'But why are you leaving in such a hurry?'

I shut my suitcase and looked into my father's concerned eyes. It was not fair on him to leave without an explanation, but I could not tell him what had really happened. I searched for a lie that sounded as close to the truth as possible.

'I have been asked to work on an experiment,' I said at last. 'It is very important, and I must leave right away.'

'What about William?'

My blood ran cold at the mention of my brother's name. Only I knew what had become of him and it filled me with sadness, fear and shame. Tears welled in my eyes. I wiped them away. I could not tell my father of William's fate without revealing how I knew.

I picked up my case and headed for the door of our once happy home. 'I will come back as soon as this experiment is over, I promise.'

***

I returned to Ingolstadt, but I could not risk making another creature there. Instead, I decided to head to Scotland. I knew of a laboratory on a remote island that

I could hire, and where I would not be disturbed or discovered.

'Why don't I come with you?' asked Henry as I gathered my notebooks for the trip. 'I am at the end of my first semester and, Victor, I am worried about you. What with William's disappearance and this sudden offer of work in Scotland – it seems like you could do with a friend.'

semester
A half-year term in universities.

I should have turned Henry down. I should not have risked him finding out about the creature. But he was persistent, and I admit I feared being left alone to obsess about the creature.

'All right,' I said. 'If you insist, you can come with me.'

CHAPTER ELEVEN

The Orkney Islands off the north coast of Scotland were as quiet and remote as I had hoped. Henry and I hired a pretty cottage to stay in, with two bedrooms and a cosy kitchen. Henry spent his days walking, meeting the locals and sketching the beautiful Scottish scenery.

I spent my days in the laboratory with the doors and windows shut, working harder and faster than ever. The laboratory was more basic than I was used to, but it had everything I needed to make another creature.

Each evening, I joined Henry at the local inn for supper. I tried not to talk about the work I was conducting. Instead, we talked of old times as children in Geneva, and the future I imagined when I returned there. Whenever I remembered how William would not be part of that future, I fell silent. It was impossible to grieve him properly in front of Henry. Although others had begun to fear the worst about his disappearance, only I knew for sure that he would not return.

'When will your wedding

to Eliza be?' asked Henry one evening, when I had fallen into another such silence.

'I haven't even asked her to marry me yet!' I replied, forcing a laugh.

'It doesn't matter,' said Henry with a smile. 'She will say yes. Eliza has been in love with you since we were little, running around in the forests and exploring.'

My mind wandered back to those simple days. I remembered how fascinated I was by how things grew. It made me shudder to think of the terrible consequences my curiosity had led to.

'Why do you look so troubled, my friend?' asked Henry, reading my face.

'It's the experiment,' I replied truthfully. 'I want it to be over with so I can go home and start my life again.'

Henry did not ask any more questions. 'In that case, let us get you some rest so that you are fit and well to begin again tomorrow.

***

The following day, I unlocked the laboratory and stared at

the second creature I had made. It had the same sickly yellow skin and hollow-looking face as the first. I checked the weather forecast in the paper. A storm was predicted for that very evening. I needed to harness the energy of lightning to make the creature come to life. I worked all day, making sure each piece of equipment was in place.

Then, as rain started to fall and the clouds turned dark, my heart began to thump.

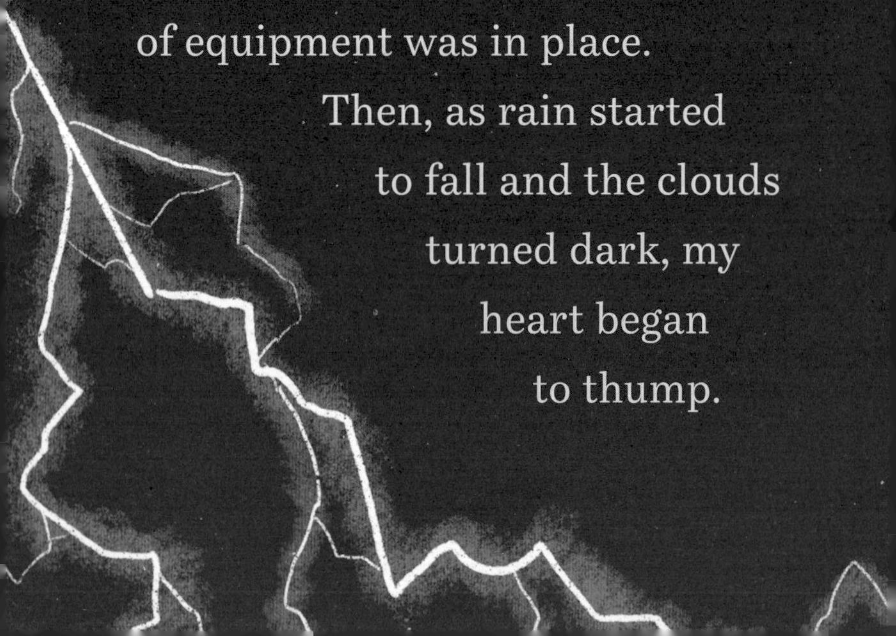

A shadow passed the window. Henry? It could not be. He would not come to visit without warning. As I stepped closer to the window, I saw that the shadow was created by someone or something unnaturally tall. As a bolt of lightning illuminated the grounds, I saw that it was the creature! It had come to meet its friend.

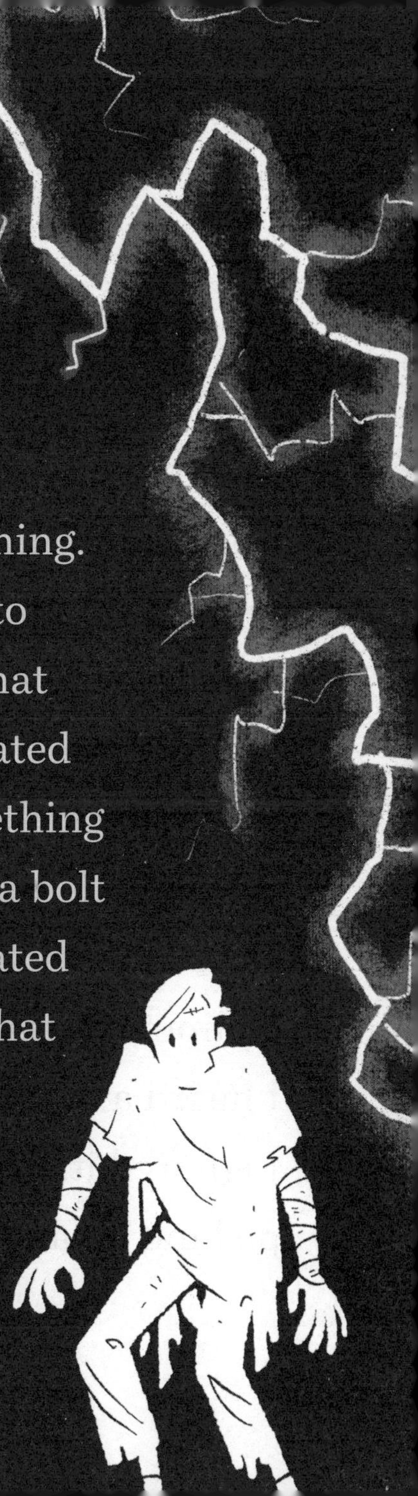

Chapter Twelve

The hideous sight of the creature was enough to shock me back into reality. What was I doing? I could not create another such monster! It was against the laws of nature and mankind. I had let my fear control me, but I had been wrong.

As I started to dismantle my equipment as quickly as I could, I heard a pounding on the door. I ignored it. The storm was picking up and I could not risk any lightning reaching my latest experiment and bringing it to life. The door crashed open.

'What are you doing?' bellowed the creature, surging through the broken doorway. 'You promised me!'

'I cannot do it!' I cried, frantically tearing my equipment apart. 'I cannot bring another monster into this world!'

As soon as my words reached the creature's ears, it stopped in its tracks. A mixture of hatred and disappointment twisted its face. 'If you do not do this, I will always be with you,' it said, slowly but with force. 'When you wake, when you sleep – when you *marry*.'

I looked away, refusing to give in to fear again, and carried on with my task. When I glanced back, the creature was gone. I did not have time to dwell on where it had disappeared to. Instead, I bundled up the second creature and dragged it outside to the beach. The storm was still raging and darkness covered the island. I was certain I would not be seen. I found a small wooden boat and rowed out to sea. When I had gone far enough, I pushed the creature over the side, into the black water.

I was exhausted, and so ashamed of myself for almost bringing another inhuman creature into the world. As I got back to the shore and stumbled into my bedroom in the cottage, I did not notice that Henry was nowhere to be seen.

***

The following morning, I awoke to a loud banging that seemed to follow me out of my nightmares.

'Open up!' shouted a voice from outside the cottage.

Still dressed in my clothes from the night before, I stumbled to the door. I recognised the island's chief police officer, with the innkeeper behind him.

'That's him! That's the man!' said the innkeeper, jabbing his finger in my direction.

'Can I help you with something, Officer?' I asked.

The police officer looked grave. 'Do you know a Mr Henry Clerval?'

'I do. Do you want me to fetch him for you?' I said, glancing back into the cottage. 'Although I think he may still be sleeping.'

'He's missing!' said the innkeeper, angrily. 'Mr Clerval comes to the inn each night at exactly the same time, waiting for you to finish doing goodness-knows-what in your lab. Last night, he did not show – and nor did you.'

Chapter Thirteen

I suddenly felt cold. Surely Henry could not be missing. I thought about William and began to tremble.

'I'm sure he just decided to spend the night at home …' I began. 'Henry!' I called. I rushed through the cottage, but Henry's room

was empty, and the bed had not been slept in. The kitchen and living room were empty too.

'He's not there,' said the innkeeper, who had followed me inside. 'Looks like he hasn't been there all night!'

'Sir,' began the police officer. 'We have a witness who says he saw you rowing out to sea with a large bundle.'

My stomach dropped when I realised what the officer was implying. 'You don't think that I killed Henry, do you?' I said, my voice shaking with fear. 'That bundle was just …' I hesitated. 'It was just some old material from my experiment.'

The police officer frowned. 'You dumped scientific material into the sea? That doesn't seem very sensible.'

I nodded, frantically searching my mind for an excuse that would sound as believable as possible. 'Yes, you see it's actually far safer to dispose of it in water.'

My breathing was rapid and my heart was thumping. Part of me was distraught, wondering what had happened to Henry; and part of me was trying to convince these men that I had not killed him.

'I'm sorry, sir, you will need to come to the station with me,' the police officer said, grabbing my arm and pulling me towards him. I had no energy to resist after the stress of the previous evening – or the previous weeks. I had barely

eaten, rarely slept. These facts seemed to catch up with me all at once.

'But it wasn't …' I began, my words catching in my throat. 'I don't know where …' I felt dizzy, my knees buckling underneath me. 'Please, you need to look for Henry … the creature … it's …'

Then everything went black.

Chapter Fourteen

I awoke in the cottage. I could hear the sea lapping against the shore and the crackle of a fire in the fireplace. Had it been just another nightmare?

'There now, Victor. How are you feeling?' I turned to see my father sitting by my bedside. It took me a moment or two to fully realise that he was really there.

'Father,' I said, my voice weak. I tried to sit up, but my arms would not lift my weight.

'Don't try to move,' he said. 'You've been asleep for days. You need time to feel strong again.' Father helped me to sip some water.

'What are you doing here?' I asked at last.

Father sighed heavily and got up to stoke the fire. 'I had a telegram from the police officer who arrested you,' he began. 'He told me you had fallen into a fever and were very ill. He said that you kept talking in your sleep about a monster.'

I swallowed as the memories of that night came flooding back. It had not been a nightmare, then.

'The chief was worried about you,' Father continued. 'He also didn't believe that you could have killed Henry. There was no real proof, after all.'

'Henry!' I said. 'Where is he?'

Father looked pale and serious. 'They found him on the cliffs,' he

replied, softly. 'I am so sorry, my boy, but Henry is dead. Murdered.'

'No!' I cried, starting to weep.

'The chief knows it was not you,' Father said, pulling me towards him. 'Whoever killed him had large hands, much bigger than yours. I am here to take you home to Geneva. Some rest and a break from your work is what is needed now.'

First William, now Henry. The creature was slowly taking everyone I loved away from me. I had refused to create a friend for it, so it took my friend from me. I argued with Father to let me stay in Scotland. I wanted to find the creature and destroy it.

With a broken voice, Father said, 'I need at least one of my sons home and safe.' Hearing his words, the fight went out of me. After all I had done, I could not deny him that much.

***

A few days later, we set sail for Switzerland. I could not rest for a moment on the journey. My eyes darted this way and that, constantly looking for any sign that the creature might be following us. It was far more intelligent than I ever imagined it to be, and had stronger emotions, too. I promised myself that I would stay watchful so that it would not take another person that I loved.

In Geneva, I found some comfort in my family home and in seeing Eliza again. With each month that passed, my memories of that awful time faded and my fear lessened. We were finally able to lay William to rest, certain that even though no body had been found, he was indeed dead. We wept over him and Henry, but slowly we began to heal.

I still kept watch for the creature, though. Each night I walked in the gardens of our family home. I would tell my father and Eliza that I liked fresh air before bed, when really I was checking the trees and bushes for any sign of the monster.

I left science behind me. I could not conduct experiments without thinking of the monster I had so foolishly created. So I found a job in a local school. The innocence of the young pupils was just what I needed to forget the horrors I had experienced.

A year on, I felt happier than I had since before my mother died. I was grateful that I had been given another chance to live a good life. And so, I finally asked Eliza to marry me.

Henry was right: she said yes.

CHAPTER FIFTEEN

With sun streaming through the stained-glass windows of the church, and happy smiles on the faces of our friends and family, Eliza and I were married.

It felt like a new beginning. I could finally draw a line under the horror of the past few years and begin anew. I could not help the sadness I felt, however, whenever I thought about William and Henry, and how they should have shared this special day with us. Instead, they were dead – killed by the hands of my hideous creation.

I pushed the thought to the back of my mind and focussed on my new wife and the happy life we would build together.

While the wedding party was still in full swing, Eliza and I set off for our honeymoon. My father had hired us a house by a lake, and I could not wait to relax by the calm shore. The house was beautiful, but a little cold. I made my way to the woodshed to gather wood for a fire, while Eliza unpacked our suitcases.

Suddenly, I heard a scream. It was Eliza. Terror ripped through me as a near-forgotten memory pushed to the front of my mind: *I will always be with you ... even when you marry.* That is what the monster had said to me the last time I saw it.

It could not be. The monster could *not* be here. Eliza screamed again, and I rushed back into the house. Relief flooded through me as I saw Eliza sitting on the bed. It faded when I realised that she could not breathe over her panic.

'What is it, my love? What did you see?'

Eliza gasped and sobbed. 'A m-monster!'

'You're safe now, breathe.'

I put my arms around her, rocking her back and forth like a child. 'Just breathe.'

Eliza breathed, but she never spoke again. The horror of the creature was too much for her to bear. Although it had not killed her, the encounter had scarred Eliza forever. I had lost my poor wife – if not in body, then in mind. It was worse than death, really: it was *living* death.

All the fear I had felt towards my creature turned to anger. It had hurt nearly all the people I cared about, and it was never going to stop. Now, neither would I.

Not until I had rid the world of it for good.

***

While my father cared for Eliza, I set off in search of the monster. I knew it liked to hide in the woods, but it also never strayed far from people, so I searched around woodmen's cottages and farms. Sure enough, I found large footprints and the remains of food and campfires.

I tracked the monster to the seashore and guessed that it had snuck onto a ship. I hired a small fishing boat and took off to sea, heading for the nearest sailing ship on the horizon. I was tired but determined. As I sailed further and further out, the sky became darker and the air colder. Chunks of ice formed on the surface of the water, and I found it hard to breathe in the sharp, freezing air. When I did, it pierced my lungs. I felt myself growing weaker.

It was then that I finally reached the ship and was helped

on board by *you*, Captain Walton.

Thank you for listening to me. Until now, I have been too scared to share my story for fear that people would despise me for my experiments. But now I need to tell the truth. If I cannot shake this illness and kill the monster, if this is the end of my story – please share it with others.

Let it be a warning to all to never play God.

EPILOGUE

Captain Walton's Story

It was a bitterly cold night when I pulled Victor Frankenstein out of his small fishing boat to board my ship. He was suffering from hypothermia. The ship's doctor immediately put him to bed, where I visited him later that night. It was then that he told me this strange story. As you can

hypothermia
A dangerous drop in body temperature. The body loses heat faster than it can produce it.

imagine, I found it hard to believe. In fact, I put it down to the illness he was suffering from; I thought it must have been playing tricks with his mind. It was not until I saw the creature with my own eyes that I truly believed.

The following evening, the ship's doctor told me that Frankenstein was dying. When I opened the door to his cabin, I saw a large figure next to his bed, weeping over the dead body. I did not recognise the figure as one of my crew,

and when they turned, I knew at once that it was the creature Frankenstein had described. It had the same yellow skin and eyes he spoke of. I was terrified when the creature stood up to its full height, filling the small cabin. It spoke to me in a rasping voice.

'He was my creator,' it said. 'I only ever wanted him to love me.'

I slammed the door to the cabin and ran back on deck, gathering as many of my crew as I could. But when we returned to the cabin, the creature was gone, never to be seen again, though I believe he is out there still. In that, Frankenstein has had his revenge – not in the creature's death, but in its long and lonely life.

For my part, I feel sorry for both Frankenstein *and* his creature. To this day, I cannot tell who was the real monster – the creator or the creation. I can only tell their story.

Now you can tell it too, and take from it what lessons you will.

AUTHOR BIOGRAPHY

MARY SHELLEY

Mary Shelley was born in London in 1797. She began *Frankenstein* in 1816 in competition with her husband, Percy, and his friend, Lord Byron, to see who could write the best horror story. Eighteen-year-old Shelley won – at a time when women were not meant to be writers. *Frankenstein* explores life, death and man versus nature. It reflects Shelley's feelings of loneliness and rejection.